for Janet and Gerald

Ω

Published by
Peachtree Publishers
1700 Chattahoochee Avenue
Atlanta, Georgia 30318-2112
www.peachtree-online.com

Text and illustrations copyright © 2001 by Ken Brown

First published in Great Britain in 2001 by Andersen Press
First US edition published in 2001 by Peachtree Publishers
First trade paperback edition published in 2015

Color separated in Switzerland by Photolitho AG, Zürich
Printed and bound in March 2018 in the United States of America by Worzalla in Stevens Point, Wisconsin

10 9 8 7 6 (hardcover)
10 9 8 7 6 5 4 3 2 (trade paperback)

HC ISBN: 978-1-56145-250-7
PB ISBN: 978-1-56145-891-2

Library of Congress Cataloging-in-Publication Data

Brown, Ken (Ken James)
What's the time, Grandma Wolf? / written and illustrated by Ken Brown.—1st ed.
p. cm.
Summary: A group of brave, or foolhardy, little animals creeps
closer and closer to Grandma Wolf as she gets down the stewpot, chops wood,
lights a fire, and prepares to fix dinner, with a surprising outcome.
ISBN 978-1-56145-250-7
[1. Wolves—Fiction. 2. Animals—Fiction.] I. Title
PZ7.B8157 Wh 2001
[E]—dc21
2001002263

What's the Time, GRANDMA WOLF?

KEN BROWN

PEACHTREE
ATLANTA

There's a wolf in the woods,
and everyone said,

"She's big and she's bad, she's old
and she's hairy. Best leave her alone,
she's mean and she's SCARY!"

But we wanted to know,
so we crept a bit closer...

and Piglet, who's brave, shouted...

"WHAT'S THE TIME, GRANDMA WOLF?"
And she opened her eyes—they were very,
very big—and yawned, "It's time I got up."

So we crept a bit closer, and Fawn, who's shy,
whispered, "What's the time, Grandma Wolf?"
And she pricked up her ears—
they were very, very big—and said,
"It's time I brushed my teeth."

So we crept a bit closer, and Crow,
who is noisy, squawked, "What's the
time, Grandma Wolf?"
And she took down a kettle—
it was very, very big—and said,
"It's time I scrubbed the stewpot."

So we crept a bit closer, and Squirrel,
who's sassy, squeaked, "What's the time,
Grandma Wolf?"
And she fetched a sharp axe—
it was very, very big—and said,
"It's time to chop the wood."

So we crept a bit closer, and Badger, who's bold,
barked, "What's the time, Grandma Wolf?"
And she picked up two pails—they were very, very
big—and said, "It's time I fetched some water."

So we crept a bit closer, and Duckling, who's silly,
quacked, "What's the time, Grandma Wolf?"
And she looked down her nose—
it was very, very big—and said,
"It's time to light the fire!"

So we crept even closer, and Rabbit, who's reckless, giggled, "What's the time, Grandma Wolf?"

So we all settled down
to a vegetable stew, and old
Grandma Wolf, what did she do?

She read us
our favorite story!